Annalena McAfee
and
Anthony Browne

KIRSTY KNOWS BEST

A Magnet Book

rincess Kirsty stirs in bed
And tries to plan the day ahead.
Should she rush to the Royal Stables?
Or help Cook lay the breakfast tables?
Should she joke with the Royal Fool?
Or call in at the Palace School?
Should she play with her favourite toys?
But, hark! What's that horrendous noise . . . ?

"Kirsty! KIRSTY! Come down and have your breakfast or you'll be late for school."
Mum's voice was shriller than an alarm clock.
Shivering, Kirsty left her warm bed and dressed for school.

"Stop your daydreaming," said Mrs. Little.
"How many times do I have to tell you, you'll be
late for school if you don't hurry up?"
But Kirsty's mind was elsewhere . . .

ost people wait till Christmas
For a feast as good as this.
But every day in Kirsty's house
There's a meal too good to miss.
With jellies, cakes, and pink ice-cream,
And other tempting food,
There are funny hats and paper chains
To get you in the mood.
It's just the thing to set you up
Before you start the day.
Breakfast time is party time
When Kirsty has her way.

Although Kirsty had a long walk to school,
she was never bored.

Sometimes Nora Nelson, the school bully,
leaned out of the window of her mother's car
and sneered, "Get a move on, slowcoach, or you'll
be late for school again."
But Kirsty wasn't listening . . .

s far as modes of transport go
A horse is quite divine,
And coaches have a special charm,
Sedan chairs, too, are fine.
But Kirsty's favourite is quite plain;
Instead of horse, or coach, or train,
To get round town she does adore her
Little rickshaw pulled by Nora.

After Kirsty had gone to school, her mum went
to work in a local supermarket.

Mrs. Little said the only outing she ever had was
her monthly visit to town for a shampoo and set.
But Kirsty knew better . . .

he crowds are hushed,
The band strikes up,
Then everybody cheers
As, dressed in glittering finery,
The guest artiste appears.
Her fame has spread
Throughout the world,
They come from near and far,
To hear the golden singing of
Joyce Little, Superstar.

Kirsty's dad, Reg, didn't have to get up early every morning. He didn't have a job.

In the evenings, when Kirsty and her mum were
home, he liked to potter about in the tool shed.
At least that's what he said he did.
But Kirsty knew better . . .

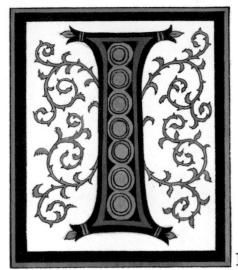

In his secret lab in the garden shed,
He pushes the frontiers of science ahead.
His latest scheme sent the town agog
When he unleashed Fido the Flying Dog.
Not content with this small operation,
He's set his heart on world domination.

Days at Kingly Junior School seemed endless.
All the children, especially Nora, thought that
playtime was too short and lessons too long.
But not Kirsty.

While the teacher droned on and on,
Kirsty was far away. . .

"Kirsty! KIRSTY! Repeat what I just said!"
But she never could.

At playtime, Kirsty was always left out. Nora
made sure of that.
But Kirsty didn't mind.

One day, Nora turned on Kirsty.
"You spend so much time daydreaming, you
look like a sleepwalker. Wakey, WAKEY!"

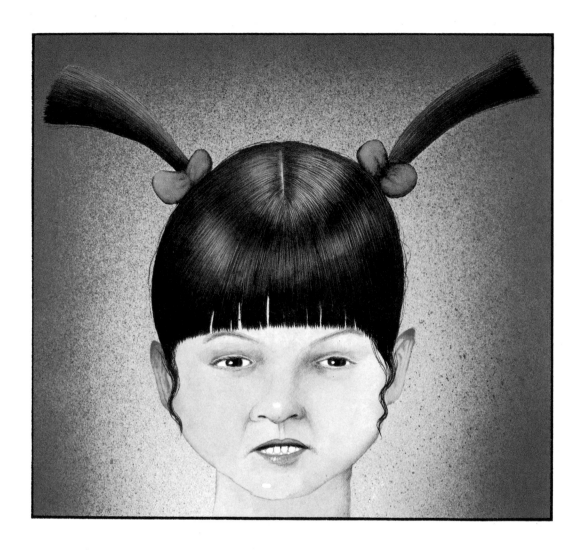

"Wakey, WAKEY! Your mum's a drudge, your dad's a slob and you're as thick as an outsize brick." But Kirsty wasn't upset. She knew better . . .

s Nasty Nora sneers and puffs
The strangest thing takes place.
Her body swells, her eyes grow large
And dwarf her little face.

he turns bright green
And then is seen
To turn into a toad.
And everyone is open-mouthed
To see the toad . . .

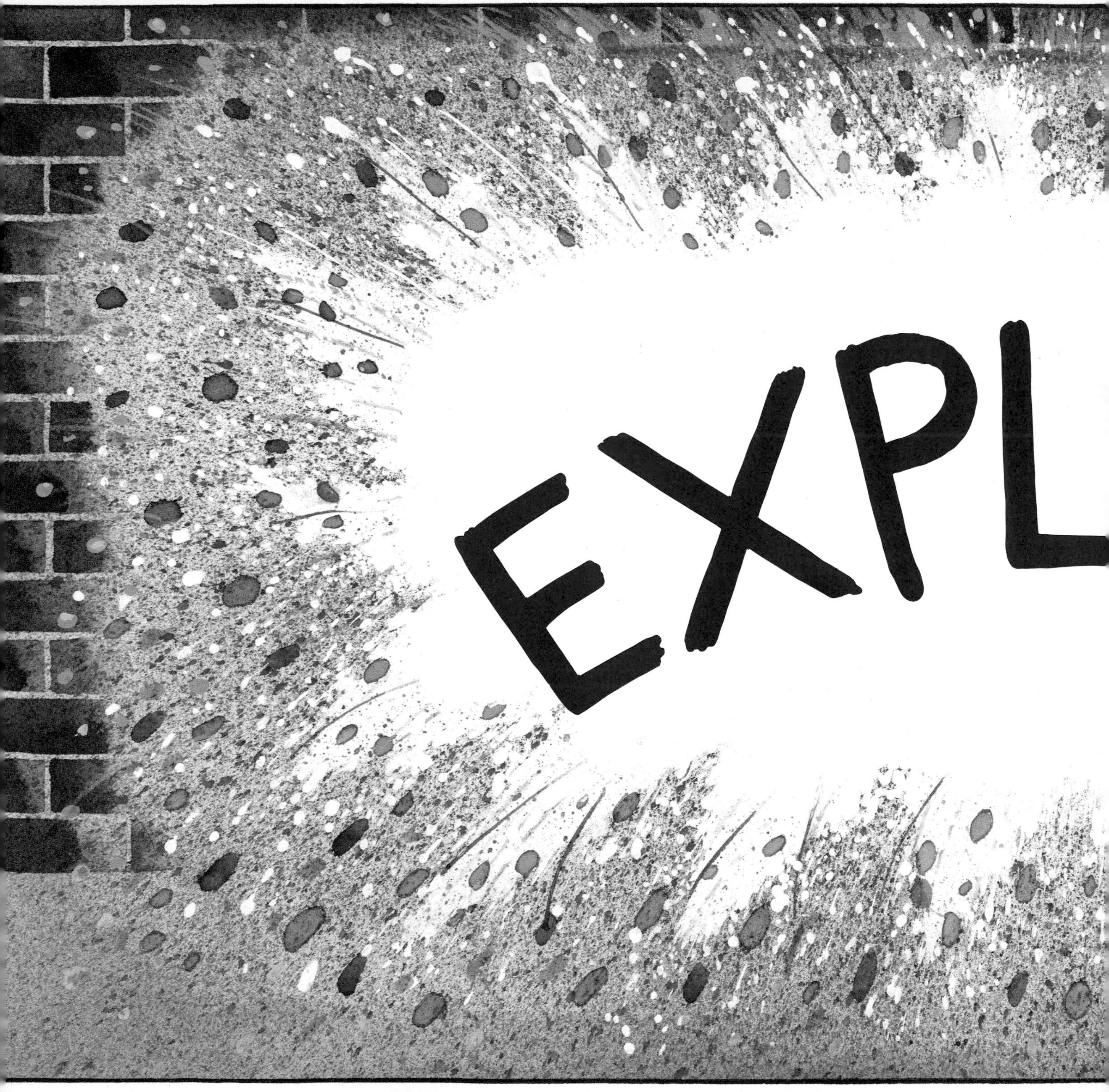
EXPL

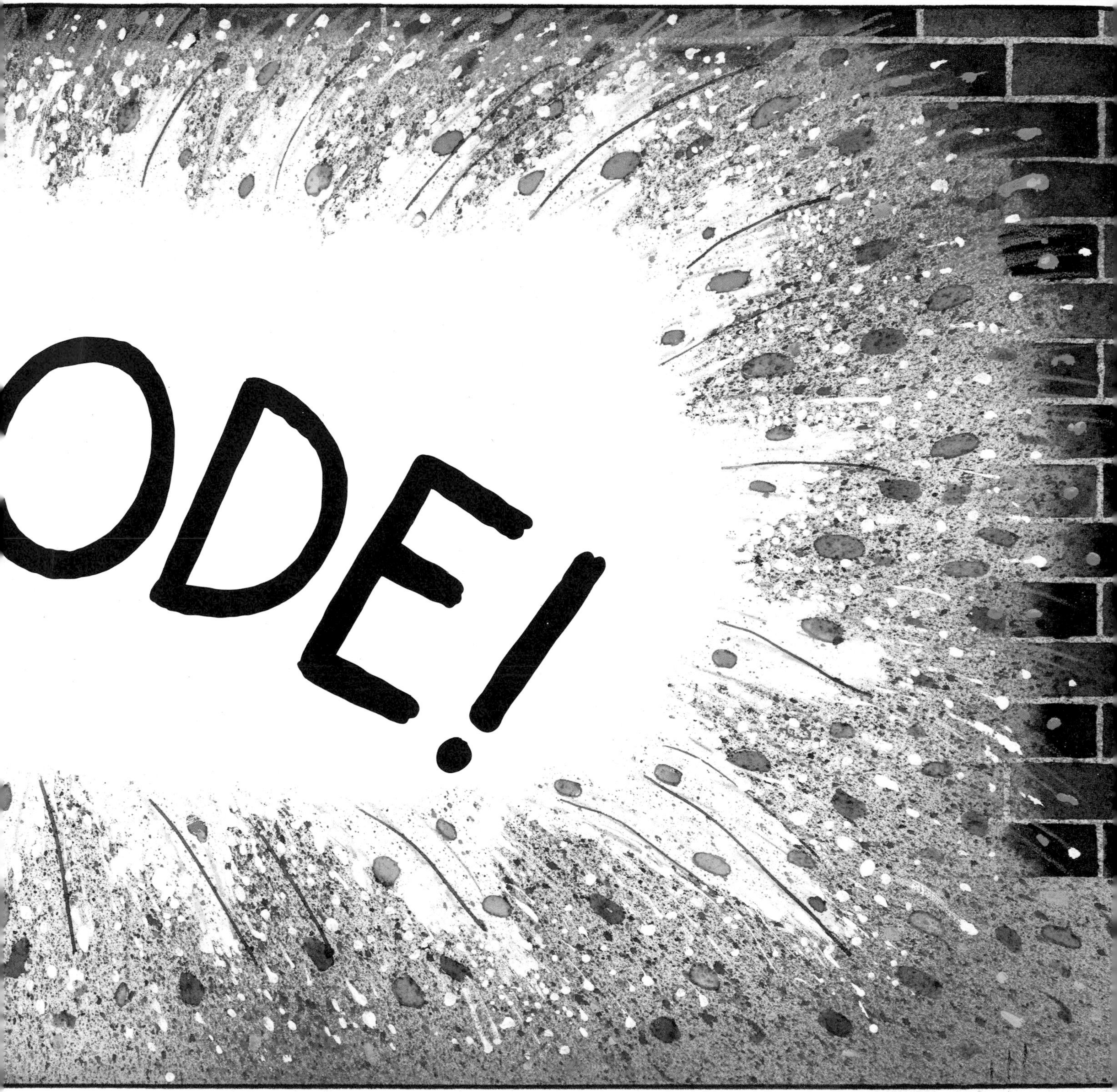
ODE!

But Kirsty knows better . . .

First published in Great Britain 1987 by Julia MacRae Books
This Magnet edition published 1988 by Methuen Children's Books
A Division of the Octopus Group Ltd
Michelin House, 81 Fulham Road, London SW3 6RB
Text copyright © 1987 Annalena McAfee
Illustrations copyright © 1987 Anthony Browne
Printed in Great Britain by Scotprint Ltd, Musselburgh

ISBN 0 416 09202 0